100 FACTS
Reptiles & Amphibians

100 FACTS
Reptiles & Amphibians

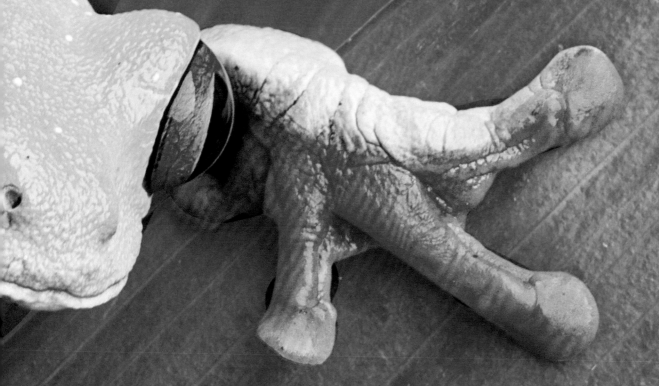

Ann Kay

Consultant: Camilla de la Bédoyère

Miles Kelly

First published in 2001 by Miles Kelly Publishing Ltd
Harding's Barn, Bardfield End Green, Thaxted, Essex, CM6 3PX

This edition updated 2014, printed 2022

12 14 16 18 20 19 17 15 13

Publishing Director Belinda Gallagher
Creative Director Jo Cowan
Editorial Director Rosie Neave
Senior Editor Sarah Parkin
Designers D&A Design, Rob Hale
Image Manager Liberty Newton
Indexer Jane Parker
Production Jennifer Brunwin
Reprographics Stephan Davis
Assets Lorraine King

ISBN 978-1-78989-266-6

Printed in China

British Library Cataloguing-in-Publication Data
A catalogue record for this book is available from the British Library

ACKNOWLEDGEMENTS
The publishers would like to thank the following sources for the use of their photographs:
Key: t = top, b = bottom, c = centre, l = left, r = right, bg = background, rt = repeated throughout

Cover (front) Chris Mattison/FLPA, (wavy lines) A.Rom/ShutterstockPremier, (back) Brandon Alms/Shutterstock
Ardea 18(tc) Ken Lucas **FLPA** 9(table br) Michael & Patricia Fogden/Minden Pictures; 10–11(bg) Fred Bavendam/Minden Pictures;
13(bl) Emanuele Biggi; 15(t) Bruno Cavignaux/Biosphoto; 34(bg) Tui De Roy/Minden Pictures; 36–37(bg) Pete Oxford/Minden
Pictures; 41(bg) Piotr Naskrecki/Minden Pictures; 44–45(bg) Cyril Ruoso/Minden Pictures; 46–47(bg) Nicolas-Alain Petit/Biosphoto;
47(tl) IMAGEBROKER,INGO SCHULZ/Imagebroker **Fotolia** 8(table tr) Becky Stares, (table cl) reb, (table bl) Eric Gevaert,
(table br) SLDigi; 11(panel tr) & 27(panel tl) Alexey Khromushin; 13(tl) Shane Kennedy; 21(panel cl) Konstantin Sutyagin;
37(panel tr) Irochka **Getty** 26(t) Gary Meszaros/Visuals Unlimited; 38(bl) David A. Northcott/Corbis Documentary
NPL 16(tr) Jurgen Freund; 17(b) Laurie Campbell; 21(b) Russell Cooper; 23(br) Dave Watts; 28(c) Tim MacMillan/John Downer Pro;
29(bg) Stephen Dalton; 32–33(bg) Bence Mate; 36(cl) Michael Richards/John Downer; 42(bl) John Cancalosi; 47(br) Visuals Unlimited
Photoshot 12(bl), 30(bg) & 39(t) NHPA **Shutterstock** 1, 6–7 & 41(bg) Eric Isselee; 2–3 & 5 Dirk Ercken; 7(t) Anneka; 8(bg) Joe
Farah; 9(table t) Dirk Ercken, (table cl) Brandon Alms, (table cr) Salim October, (table bl) Jason Mintzer, (bg) aaltair; 11(tr) iliuta goean;
12(paper br rt) monbibi; 12–13(bg) Brian Lasenby; 15(bl) AdStock RF; 17(panel tr) Fat Jackey; 18–19 Meister Photos; 19(chameleon)
Brandon Alms, (tree frog) kyslynskahal; 21(tr) infografick; 22(br) Manja; 23(tr) clearviewstock; 24(b) Statsenko 24–25(bg) Ivan Kuzmin;
25(b) Anneka; 26(bl) Cathy Keifer; 27(bg) worldswildlifewonders; 28(b) Madlen; 28–29(bg) Iakov Kalinin; 30(bl) J. L. Levy; 35(bg) Rich
Carey; 40(bg) alslutsky; 43(bl) Audrey Snider-Bell **Superstock** 20(l) Animals Animals

All other photographs are from: Digital Vision, PhotoDisc

All artworks are from the Miles Kelly Artwork Bank

Every effort has been made to acknowledge the source and copyright holder of each picture.
Miles Kelly Publishing apologizes for any unintentional errors or omissions.

Made with paper from a sustainable forest

www.mileskelly.net

Contents

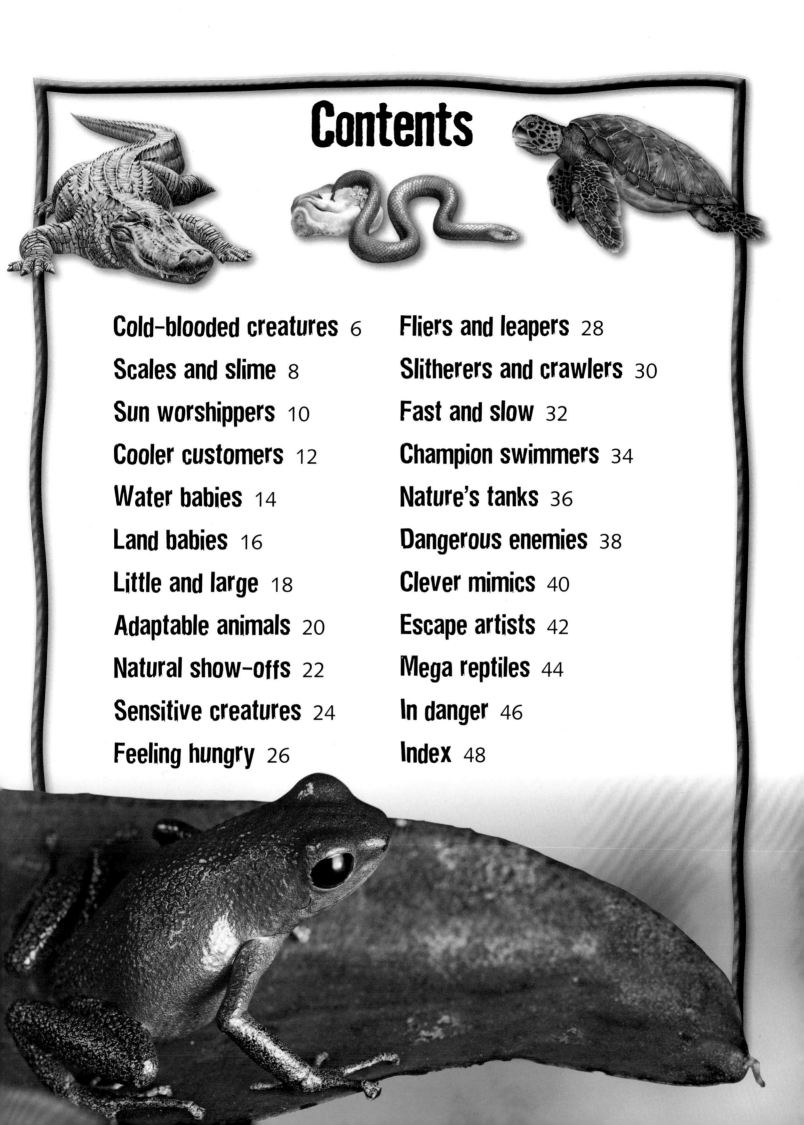

Cold-blooded creatures

1 Reptiles and amphibians are cold-blooded animals. This means that they need the Sun's heat to warm them up. Reptiles spend much of their time on land, but most amphibians live in or around water.

Ear

Dry, scaly skin

Sharp claws

▶ The skin of an amphibian is smooth and moist. Most amphibians, such as this frog, have long hind legs that are ideal for jumping.

Smooth, moist skin

Large eyes

Long hind legs

Long toes

Four legs

Long tail

Four legs

◀ Reptiles, such as this lizard, have dry, scaly skin and are often colourful creatures. Not all reptiles have legs, but if they do, their legs are on the sides of their bodies.

Scales and slime

2 **Reptiles and amphibians can be divided into smaller groups.** There are four kinds of reptiles – snakes, lizards and amphisbaenians, the crocodile family, tortoises and turtles, and the tuataras. Amphibians are split into frogs and toads, newts and salamanders, and caecilians.

3 **Reptiles do a lot of sunbathing!** Sitting in the sun is called basking – reptiles bask to warm themselves with the Sun's heat so they can move. When it gets cold, at night or during a cold season, reptiles might hibernate, which is a type of deep sleep.

▶ Blue-collared lizards may bask for many hours at a time.

Reptile family

Over half of all reptiles are lizards – there are nearly 5000 species.

Amphisbaenians, or worm lizards, are burrowing reptiles that live underground.

Tuataras are rare, ancient and unusual reptiles from New Zealand.

Snakes are the second largest group of reptiles.

Crocodiles, alligators, gharials and caimans are predators with sharp teeth.

Turtles and tortoises have hard shells that protect them from predators.

4 **Most reptiles have dry, scaly, waterproof skin.** This stops their bodies from drying out. The scales are made of keratin and may form thick, tough plates. Human nails are made of the same material.

Amphibian family

Newts have slender bodies and long tails.

Frogs have smooth skin and long legs for jumping.

Toads often have warty skin and crawl or walk.

Salamanders have tails and they usually have bright markings.

Caecilians are burrowing animals without legs.

▼ Green-skinned frogs can hide among leaves and pondweed.

5 Amphibians have skin that is moist, smooth and soft. Oxygen can pass easily through their skin, which is important because most adult amphibians breathe through their skin as well as with their lungs. Reptiles breathe only with their lungs.

6 Amphibians' skin is kept moist by special glands just under the surface. These glands produce a sticky substance called mucus. Many amphibians also keep their skin moist by making sure that they are never far away from water.

7 Some amphibians have no lungs. Humans breathe with their lungs to get oxygen from the air and breathe out carbon dioxide. Most amphibians breathe through their skin and lungs, but lungless salamanders breathe only through their skin and the lining of the mouth.

QUIZ
1. Why do reptiles bask?
2. How do most amphibians breathe?
3. How do reptiles breathe?

Answers:
1. To warm themselves with the Sun's heat so they can move
2. Through their skin and with their lungs 3. With their lungs

9

Sun worshippers

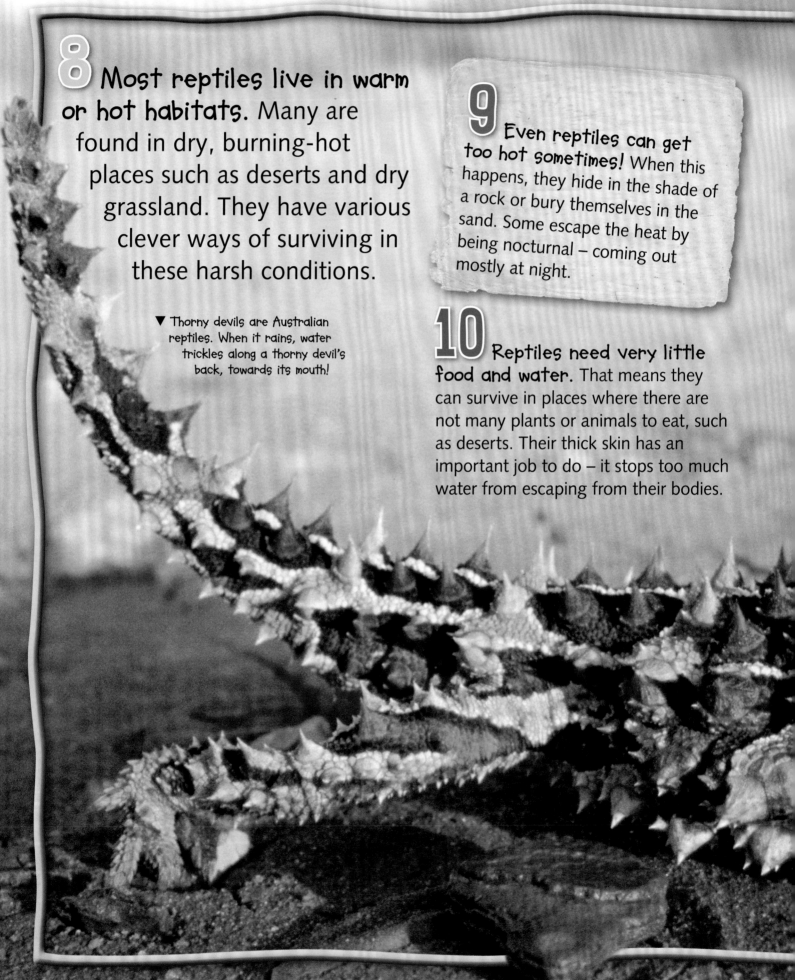

8 Most reptiles live in warm or hot habitats. Many are found in dry, burning-hot places such as deserts and dry grassland. They have various clever ways of surviving in these harsh conditions.

▼ Thorny devils are Australian reptiles. When it rains, water trickles along a thorny devil's back, towards its mouth!

9 Even reptiles can get too hot sometimes! When this happens, they hide in the shade of a rock or bury themselves in the sand. Some escape the heat by being nocturnal – coming out mostly at night.

10 Reptiles need very little food and water. That means they can survive in places where there are not many plants or animals to eat, such as deserts. Their thick skin has an important job to do – it stops too much water from escaping from their bodies.

▲ A spadefoot toad has strong, clawed feet for digging.

11 Reptiles need a certain level of warmth to survive. This is why there are no reptiles in very cold places, such as at the North and South Poles, or at the very tops of mountains.

12 Like reptiles, many amphibians live in very hot places. Sometimes it can get too hot and dry for them. The spadefoot toad from Europe, Asia and North America buries itself in the sand to escape the heat and dryness.

I DON'T BELIEVE IT!

The sand lizard of the African Namib Desert performs strange dances. When it gets too hot, it may lift its legs up and down off the burning sand, or lie on its stomach and raise all its legs at once!

Cooler customers

13 Many amphibians are common in cooler, damper parts of the world. Amphibians like wet places. Most mate and lay their eggs in water.

▶ Frogs can hide from strong sunlight by resting in trees or under plants.

14 As spring arrives, amphibians come out of hiding. The warmer weather sees many amphibians returning to the pond or stream where they were born. This may mean a very long journey through towns or over busy roads.

◀ Wildlife watchers help common toads cross the road to reach their breeding ponds in safety.

▲ When it is time to hibernate, a frog must find a safe, damp place to stay.

I DON'T BELIEVE IT!

In some countries, signs warn drivers of a very unusual 'hazard' ahead – frogs or toads travelling along the roads to return to breeding grounds.

15 When the weather turns especially cold, amphibians often hide away. They simply hibernate in the mud at the bottom of ponds or under stones and logs. This means that they go to sleep in the autumn and don't wake up until spring.

Gills

▶ This is a mudpuppy – a type of salamander. It spends its whole life underwater and breathes using its frilly gills.

▲ Pygmy marbled newts avoid getting too hot by hiding under rotting wood or by resting in mud during the day.

16 Journeys to breeding grounds may be up to 5 kilometres – a long way for an animal only a few centimetres in length. This is like a person walking 90 kilometres away without a map! The animals find their way by scent, landmarks, the Earth's magnetic field and the Sun's position.

Water babies

17 Amphibians live in water and on land. Most are born and grow up in fresh water such as ponds, pools, streams and rivers. They move onto dry land when they are adults and return to water to breed.

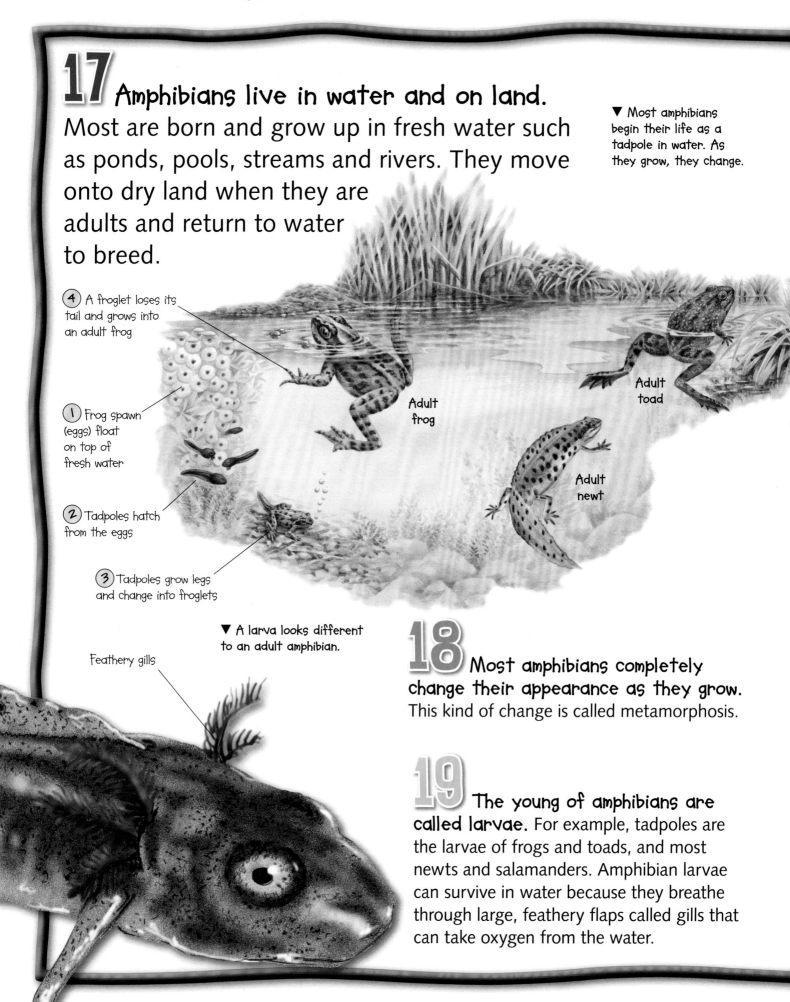

▼ Most amphibians begin their life as a tadpole in water. As they grow, they change.

④ A froglet loses its tail and grows into an adult frog

① Frog spawn (eggs) float on top of fresh water

② Tadpoles hatch from the eggs

③ Tadpoles grow legs and change into froglets

Adult frog

Adult toad

Adult newt

▼ A larva looks different to an adult amphibian.

Feathery gills

18 Most amphibians completely change their appearance as they grow. This kind of change is called metamorphosis.

19 The young of amphibians are called larvae. For example, tadpoles are the larvae of frogs and toads, and most newts and salamanders. Amphibian larvae can survive in water because they breathe through large, feathery flaps called gills that can take oxygen from the water.

▲ An axolotl is a strange creature that remains a tadpole all its life.

20 **The axolotl is an amphibian that has never grown up.** This type of water-living salamander has never developed beyond the larval stage. It does, however, develop far enough to be able to breed.

▼ Toads can lay hundreds — even thousands — of eggs at a time.

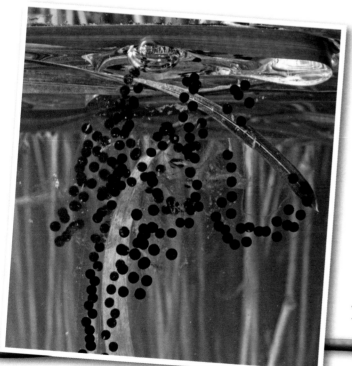

I DON'T BELIEVE IT!

The male South American Surinam toad is quite an acrobat. When mating underwater, it has to press the eggs onto its mate's back. The eggs remain there until they hatch.

21 **The majority of amphibians lay soft eggs.** These may be in a jelly-like string or clump of tiny eggs called spawn, as with frogs and toads. Newts lay their eggs singly.

22 **A few amphibians give birth to live young instead of laying eggs.** The eggs of the fire salamander, for example, stay inside their mother, where the young hatch out and develop. The female then gives birth to young that are like miniature adults.

Land babies

23 The majority of reptiles spend their whole lives away from water. They are very well adapted for life on dry land. Some do spend time in the water, but most reptiles lay their eggs on land.

▶ A leatherback turtle uses her hind legs to dig a burrow in the sand, and then lays her clutch of round eggs inside.

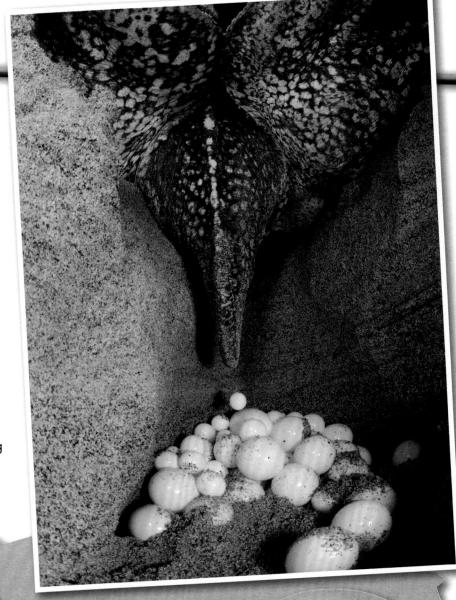

Alligator

Ground python

Javan bloodsucker lizard

Galapagos giant tortoise

▲ Reptiles lay eggs of different shapes and sizes.

24 Most reptile eggs are much tougher than those of amphibians. This is because they must survive life out of the water. Lizards and snakes lay eggs with leathery shells. Crocodile and tortoise eggs have a hard shell rather like birds' eggs.

25 The eggs feed and protect the young developing inside them. Yolk provides food for the developing young, which is called an embryo. The shell protects the embryo from the outside world, but also allows vital oxygen into the egg.

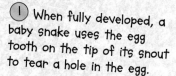

① When fully developed, a baby snake uses the egg tooth on the tip of its snout to tear a hole in the egg.

② The snake tastes the air with its forked tongue. It may stay in the shell for a few more days.

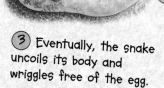

③ Eventually, the snake uncoils its body and wriggles free of the egg.

④ The baby snake slides along in S-shaped curves to begin its life in the wild.

AMAZING EGGS

Reptile eggs are like birds' eggs. Next time you eat an egg, rinse out half an empty eggshell, fill it with water and wait a while. See how no water escapes! Wash your hands well once you're done. Like this bird's eggshell, reptile eggshells stop the egg from drying out, although they let air in and are tough enough to protect the embryo.

26 Young reptiles hatch out of eggs as miniature adults. They do not undergo a change, or metamorphosis, like amphibians do.

▶ A slow worm protects her eggs inside her body, until they are ready to hatch.

27 Some snakes and lizards, like slow worms, don't lay eggs. Instead, they give birth to fully developed live young. Animals that do this are called 'viviparous'.

Little and large

28 Reptiles and amphibians come in every shape and size. There are more than 9000 species (types) of reptiles and 7000 species of amphibians. They range from tiny frogs to giant, dinosaur-like lizards.

▲ Chinese salamanders are often heavier than their Japanese cousins. They can weigh up to 65 kg – more than a child!

29 The largest reptile is the saltwater crocodile from around the Indian and west Pacific Oceans. It can grow to a staggering 7 metres from nose to tail – an average adult human is not even 2 metres tall! Japan's cold streams are home to the largest amphibian – a giant salamander that is around 1.5 metres in length and weighs up to 40 kilograms.

▼ Most saltwater crocodiles grow to be about 5 metres in length. These massive predators are called 'salties' in Australia.

30 The world's tiniest reptiles are dwarf geckos. The smallest one discovered so far measured just 16 millimetres in length. The Brazilian gold frog is one of the smallest amphibians. Its body length is just 9.8 millimetres – that makes it small enough to sit on your thumbnail!

▶ A European tree frog is up to 50 millimetres long.

▼ A female pygmy leaf chameleon is just 34 millimetres long, but the male is even smaller!

ACTUAL SIZE

Adaptable animals

31 Many reptiles and amphibians have special adaptations to help them live safely and easily in their surroundings. For example, crocodiles have a special flap in their throats that means that they can open their mouth underwater without breathing in water.

32 Geckos can climb up vertical surfaces or even upside down. They are able to cling on because they have five wide-spreading toes, each with sticky toe-pads, on each foot. These strong pads are covered with millions of tiny hairs that grip surfaces tightly.

◄ Tokay geckos are one of the largest geckos. They can reach up to 35 centimetres in length and are usually brightly patterned.

33 Tortoises and turtles have hard, bony shells for protection. They form a suit of armour that protects them from predators and also from the hot Sun.

LEARNING MORE

Pick a favourite reptile or amphibian and then find out as much as you can about it. List all the ways you think it is especially well adapted to deal with its lifestyle and habitat.

▶ Colourful chameleons often have a row of spines on their backs to make them look fierce.

34 Chameleons have adapted well to their way of life in the trees. They have long toes that can grip branches firmly, and a long tail that grips like another hand. Tails that can grip like this are called prehensile. Chameleons are also known for being able to change their colour to blend in with their surroundings. This is called camouflage, and is something that many other reptiles and amphibians use.

35 The flattened tails of newts make them expert swimmers. Newts are salamanders that spend most of their lives in water, so they need to be able to get about speedily in this environment.

▼ The smooth newt has a flat, paddle-like tail that helps it swim quickly as it chases prey.

36 Some amphibians use gills to breathe underwater. Blood flows inside the feathery gills as water flows over the outside. As the water flows past the gills, oxygen passes out of the water, straight into the blood.

Natural show-offs

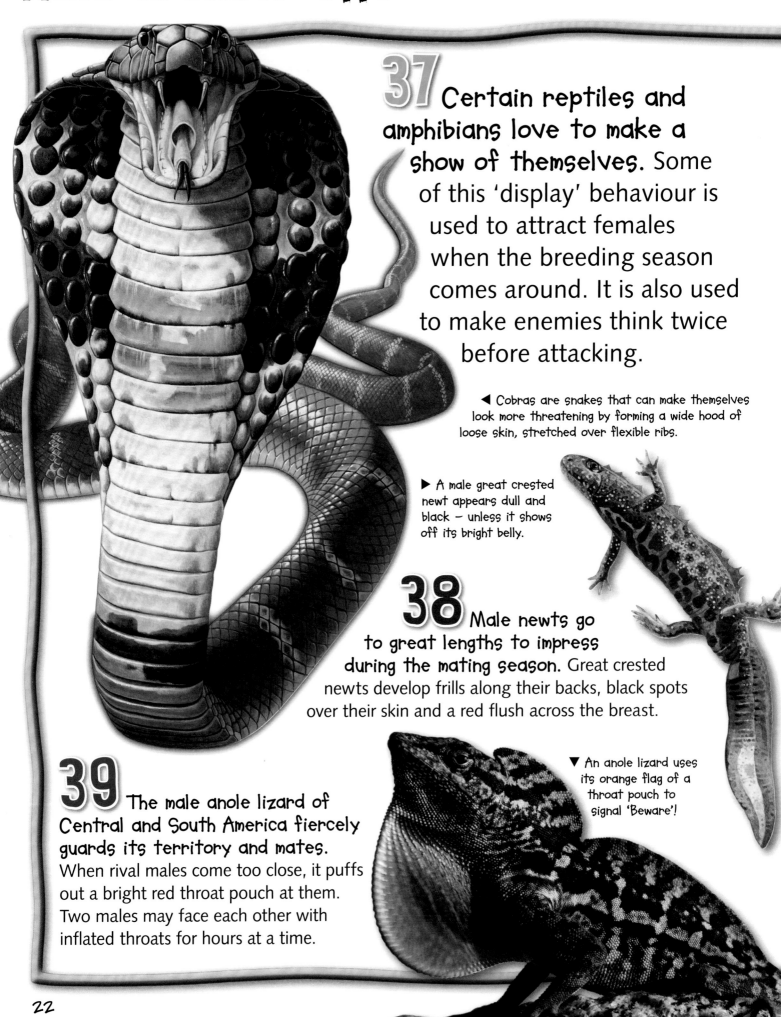

37 Certain reptiles and amphibians love to make a show of themselves. Some of this 'display' behaviour is used to attract females when the breeding season comes around. It is also used to make enemies think twice before attacking.

◀ Cobras are snakes that can make themselves look more threatening by forming a wide hood of loose skin, stretched over flexible ribs.

▶ A male great crested newt appears dull and black – unless it shows off its bright belly.

38 Male newts go to great lengths to impress during the mating season. Great crested newts develop frills along their backs, black spots over their skin and a red flush across the breast.

▼ An anole lizard uses its orange flag of a throat pouch to signal 'Beware'!

39 The male anole lizard of Central and South America fiercely guards its territory and mates. When rival males come too close, it puffs out a bright red throat pouch at them. Two males may face each other with inflated throats for hours at a time.

40 Many frogs and toads puff themselves up. Toads can inflate their bodies to appear more frightening. Frogs and toads can also puff out their throat pouches. This makes their croaking love-calls to mates and 'back off' calls to enemies much louder.

▲ A green tree frog uses its air-filled throat pouch to impress a female.

41 A frilled lizard in full display is an amazing sight. This lizard has a large flap of neck skin that normally lies flat. When faced by a predator, it spreads this out to form a huge, stiff ruff that makes the lizard look bigger and scarier!

42 Male monitor lizards have wrestling competitions! At the beginning of the mating season they compete to try to win the females. They rear up on their hind legs and wrestle until the weaker one gives up.

▲ A frilled lizard scares predators away with its huge frill, large yellow mouth and a loud hiss.

Sensitive creatures

43 Reptiles and amphibians find out about the world by using their senses, such as taste and sight. Senses tell an animal about the world around them and any deadly animals that may be lurking nearby. Good senses can also help an animal to find food and mates.

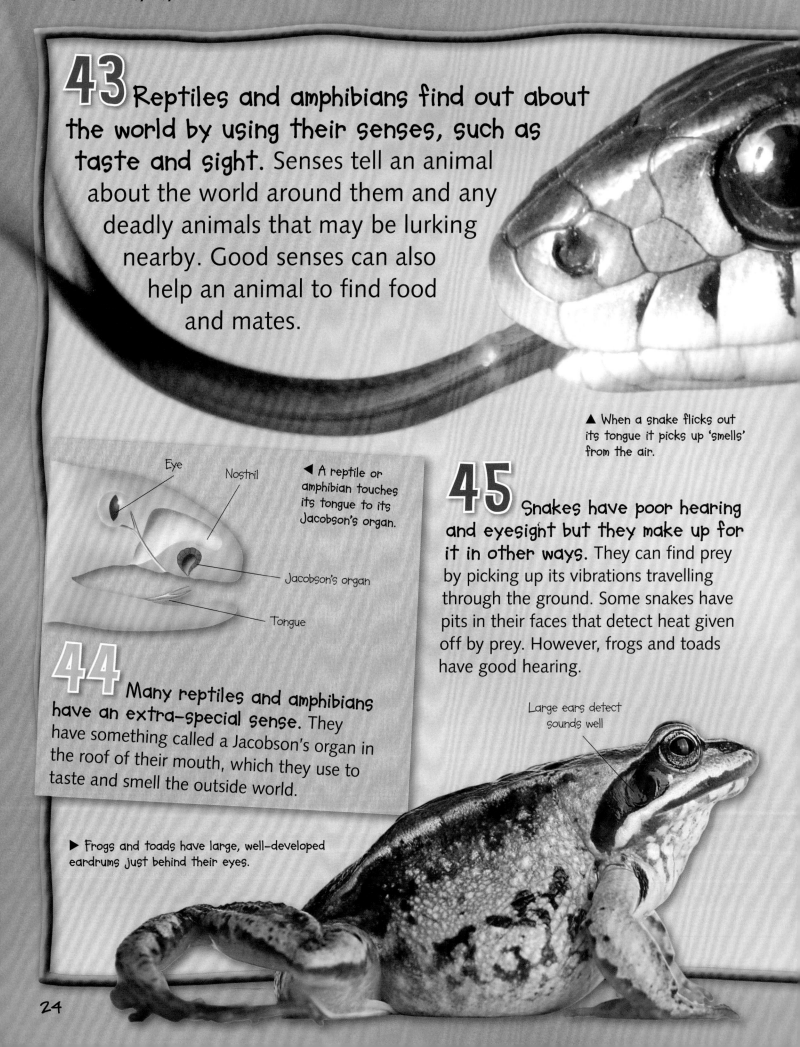

▲ When a snake flicks out its tongue it picks up 'smells' from the air.

Eye

Nostril

◄ A reptile or amphibian touches its tongue to its Jacobson's organ.

Jacobson's organ

Tongue

44 Many reptiles and amphibians have an extra-special sense. They have something called a Jacobson's organ in the roof of their mouth, which they use to taste and smell the outside world.

45 Snakes have poor hearing and eyesight but they make up for it in other ways. They can find prey by picking up its vibrations travelling through the ground. Some snakes have pits in their faces that detect heat given off by prey. However, frogs and toads have good hearing.

Large ears detect sounds well

▶ Frogs and toads have large, well-developed eardrums just behind their eyes.

24

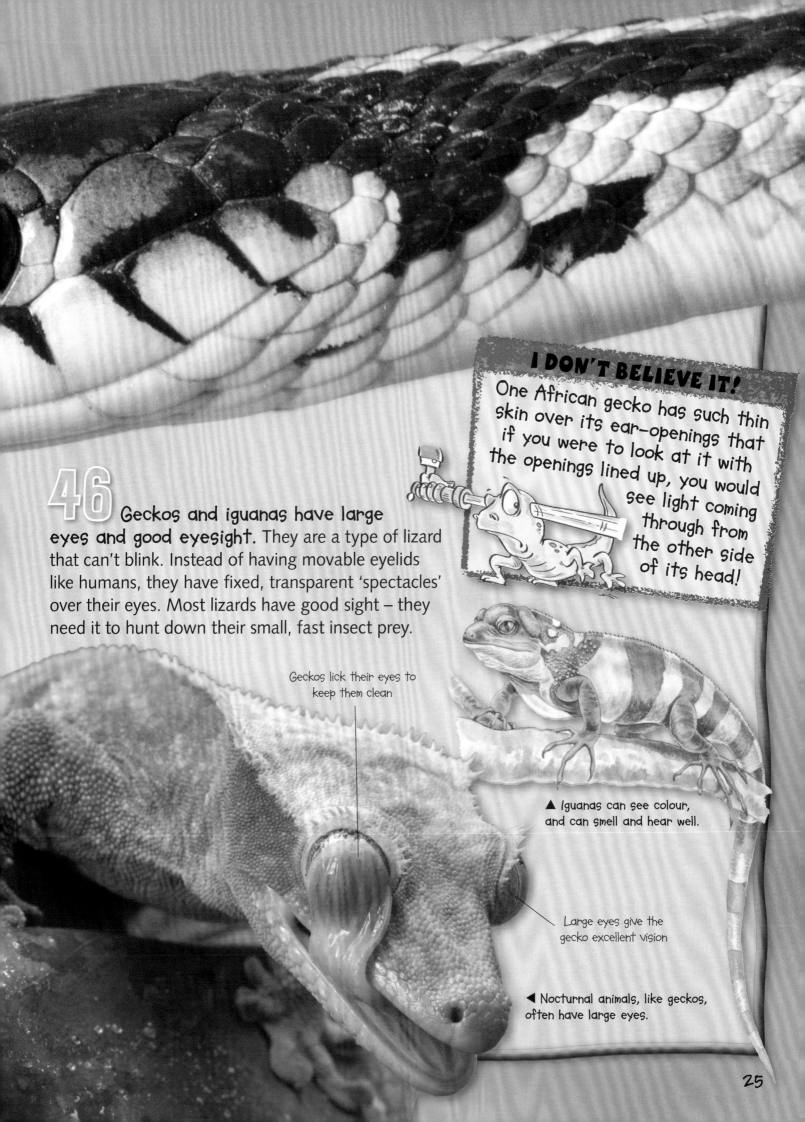

46 **Geckos and iguanas have large eyes and good eyesight.** They are a type of lizard that can't blink. Instead of having movable eyelids like humans, they have fixed, transparent 'spectacles' over their eyes. Most lizards have good sight – they need it to hunt down their small, fast insect prey.

Geckos lick their eyes to keep them clean

▲ Iguanas can see colour, and can smell and hear well.

Large eyes give the gecko excellent vision

◄ Nocturnal animals, like geckos, often have large eyes.

25

Feeling hungry

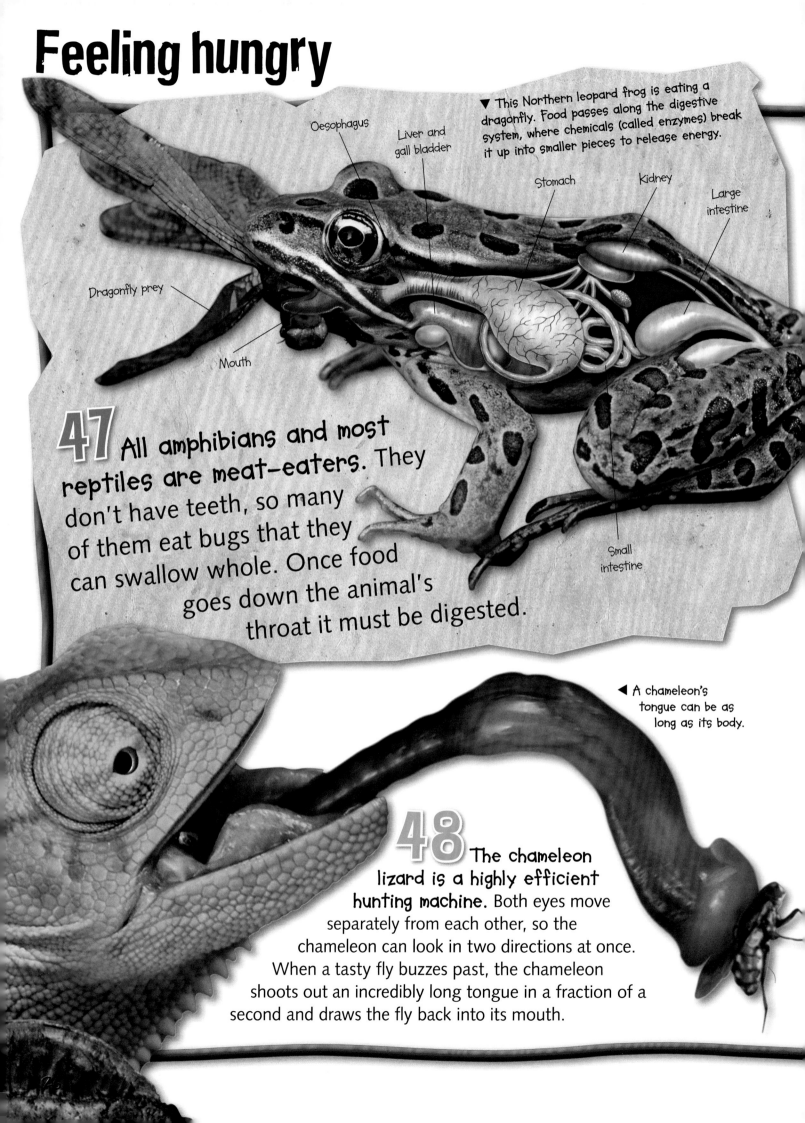

Oesophagus

Liver and gall bladder

▼ This Northern leopard frog is eating a dragonfly. Food passes along the digestive system, where chemicals (called enzymes) break it up into smaller pieces to release energy.

Stomach

Kidney

Large intestine

Dragonfly prey

Mouth

Small intestine

47 All amphibians and most reptiles are meat-eaters. They don't have teeth, so many of them eat bugs that they can swallow whole. Once food goes down the animal's throat it must be digested.

◀ A chameleon's tongue can be as long as its body.

48 The chameleon lizard is a highly efficient hunting machine. Both eyes move separately from each other, so the chameleon can look in two directions at once. When a tasty fly buzzes past, the chameleon shoots out an incredibly long tongue in a fraction of a second and draws the fly back into its mouth.

49 Salamanders creep up slowly before striking. They move gradually towards prey and then suddenly seize it with their tongue, or between their sharp teeth.

50 Large reptiles can manage massive meals! Crocodiles and big snakes open their jaws wide enough to bite animals that are as big as themselves. Crocodiles must bite lumps of meat off their prey to swallow, and they also swallow stones to help grind the food up.

◄ Crocodiles wait in shallow water for animals to come and drink, then leap up and drag their prey under the water.

BE A CHAMELEON

Like a chameleon, you need two eyes to judge distances easily. Close one eye, hold a finger out in front of you, and then try to touch this fingertip with the other. Now open both eyes and you'll find it a lot easier. Two eyes give your brain two slightly different angles to look at the object, so it is easier to tell how far away it is.

Fliers and leapers

51 Some reptiles and amphibians can take to the air — if only for a few seconds. This helps animals to travel further, escape predators or swoop down on passing prey before it gets away.

▼ A Blandford's flying lizard has thin wing-like flaps of skin that are supported by 5—7 pairs of ribs. It can travel up to 10 metres between trees.

53 Even certain kinds of snake can glide. The flying snake lives in the tropical forests of southern Asia. It can jump between branches or glide through the air in 'S' movements.

52 Reptiles that glide turn their bodies into parachutes. They are able to spread their bodies out, making them wide so they catch the air and slow their descent.

54 Flying geckos have wide, webbed feet. They use flaps of skin along their sides to help control their flight as they leap between trees. Flying geckos take to the air to avoid danger.

▼ The four webbed feet of a Wallace's flying frog help it to glide.

55 **Some frogs can glide.** Deep in the steamy rainforests of Southeast Asia and South America, tree frogs flit from tree to tree. Some can glide as far as 12 metres, clinging to their landing spot with suckers on their feet.

QUIZ

1. Where does the flying snake live?
2. How far can some tree frogs glide?
3. Which frog has been known to jump up to 4.2 metres?

Answers:
1. In the tropical forests of southern Asia 2. 12 metres 3. The rocket frog

56 **Frogs and toads use their powerful hind legs for hopping or jumping.** The greatest frog leaper comes from Africa. Known as the rocket frog, it has been known to jump up to 4.2 metres.

① The powerful muscles in the frog's hind legs push off

② In mid-leap, the frog's hind legs are fully stretched out, its front legs are held back and its eyes are closed for protection

③ As it lands, its body arches and the front legs act as a brake

Slitherers and crawlers

57 Most reptiles, and some amphibians, spend much of their time creeping, crawling and slithering along the ground. Scientists call the study of reptiles and amphibians 'herpetology', which comes from a Greek word meaning 'to creep or crawl'.

58 A snake's skin does not grow with its body. This means that it has to shed its skin to grow bigger. When a snake sheds its skin it is said to be moulting. Snakes moult at least once a year.

SLITHER AND SLIDE

Make your own slithery snake! First, collect as many cotton reels as you can, then paint them lots of bright colours. Next, cut a forked tongue and some snake eyes out of some paper. Stick them onto one of the reels to make a head. Now thread your reels onto a piece of string. Make sure the head isn't in the middle!

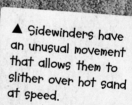

▲ Sidewinders have an unusual movement that allows them to slither over hot sand at speed.

▲ A moult begins at a snake's nose and can take up to 14 days to complete.

59 Some frogs and toads also shed their skin. The European toad sheds its skin several times during the summer – and then eats it! This recycles the goodness in the toad's skin.

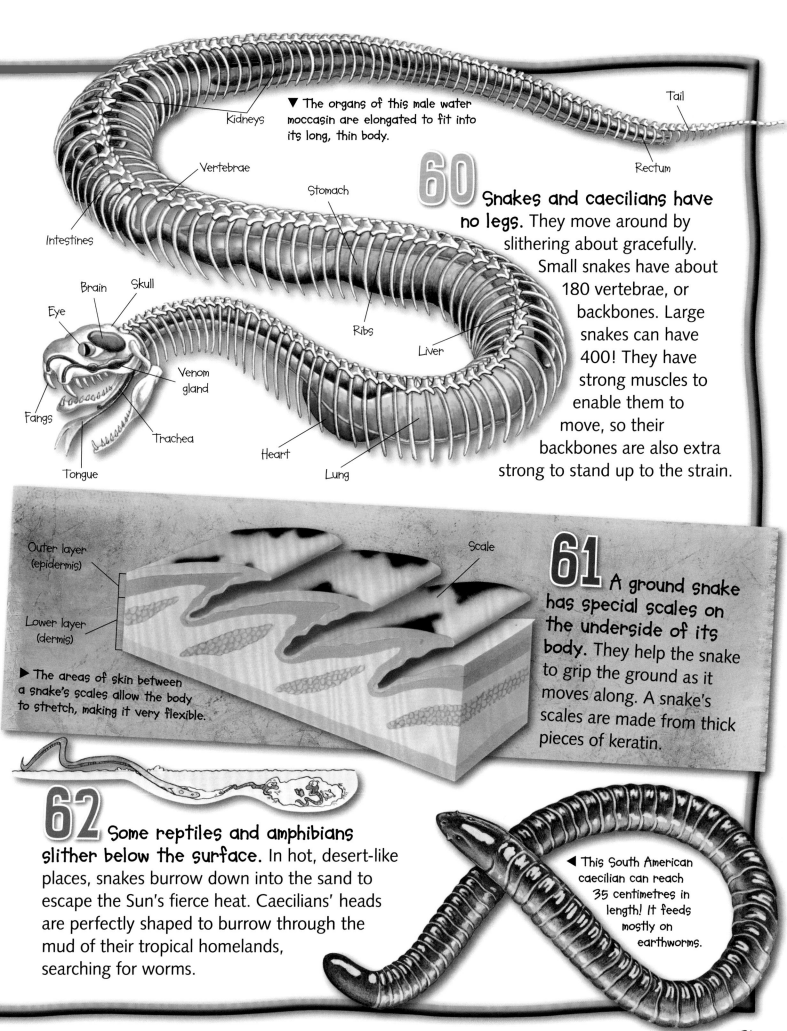

▼ The organs of this male water moccasin are elongated to fit into its long, thin body.

Tail

Rectum

Kidneys

Vertebrae

Stomach

Intestines

Brain   Skull

Eye

Ribs

Liver

Fangs

Venom gland

Trachea

Heart

Tongue

Lung

60 Snakes and caecilians have no legs. They move around by slithering about gracefully. Small snakes have about 180 vertebrae, or backbones. Large snakes can have 400! They have strong muscles to enable them to move, so their backbones are also extra strong to stand up to the strain.

Outer layer (epidermis)

Scale

Lower layer (dermis)

▶ The areas of skin between a snake's scales allow the body to stretch, making it very flexible.

61 A ground snake has special scales on the underside of its body. They help the snake to grip the ground as it moves along. A snake's scales are made from thick pieces of keratin.

62 Some reptiles and amphibians slither below the surface. In hot, desert-like places, snakes burrow down into the sand to escape the Sun's fierce heat. Caecilians' heads are perfectly shaped to burrow through the mud of their tropical homelands, searching for worms.

◀ This South American caecilian can reach 35 centimetres in length! It feeds mostly on earthworms.

Fast and slow

63 The reptile and amphibian worlds contain their fair share of fast and slow movers. However, a predator may be able to seize the slow-moving tortoise, but it will struggle to bite through its armour-plated shell!

64 Tortoises are among the slowest animals on Earth. The top speed for a giant tortoise is 5 metres a minute! These giant reptiles live on the Galapagos Islands in the Pacific Ocean and the Seychelles in the Indian Ocean.

65 Some lizards can run on water. Basilisks from Costa Rica and Philippine sail-fin water dragons leap into the water to escape from predators. They are good swimmers, but their most impressive trick is to sprint across the water's surface on their long hind legs.

◀ The enormous Galapagos giant tortoise may weigh as much as four adult humans.

FLAT RACE

Get a group of friends together and hold your own animal race day! Each of you cuts a flat animal shape – a frog or tortoise for example – out of paper or light card. Add details with coloured pencils or pens. Now race your animals along the ground to the finishing line by flapping a newspaper or a magazine behind them.

▼ A plumed basilisk uses its tail and wide feet to stay on the water's surface as it runs.

66 One of the world's slowest animals is the lizard-like tuatara. When resting, it breathes just once an hour, and may still be growing when it is 35 years old! Their slow lifestyle in part means that tuataras can live to be 120 years old.

▲ Tuataras live on a few small islands off the coast of New Zealand.

67 The fastest reptile in the world is the speedy spiny-tailed iguana. It can reach top speeds of 35 kilometres an hour. Racerunner lizards come a close second – in 1941 one of these racing reptiles ran at 29 kilometres an hour.

68 The fastest snake on land is the deadly black mamba. These shy African snakes are nervous reptiles that are easily scared – and quick to attack. This combination makes a mamba a snake to avoid!

Champion swimmers

69 Amphibians are well known for their links with water, but some types of reptile are also aquatic (live in or near water). Different types of amphibian and reptile have developed all kinds of ways of tackling watery lifestyles.

▼ Marine iguanas dive into chilly seawater to graze on seaweed. They can dive up to 9 metres at a time, but then have to bask to warm up again.

I DON'T BELIEVE IT!

Floating sea snakes can be surrounded by fish who gather at the snake's tail to avoid being eaten. When the snake fancies a snack, it swims backwards, fooling the fish into thinking its head is its tail!

70 Newts and salamanders swim rather like fish. They make an 'S' shape as they move. Many have flat tails that help to propel them through the water.

71 Toads and frogs propel themselves by kicking back with their hind legs. They use their front legs as a brake for landing when they dive into the water. Large, webbed feet act like flippers, helping them to push through the water.

1 Frog draws its legs up

3 The main kick back with toes spread propels the frog forward through the water

2 It then pushes its feet out to the side

4 Frog closes its toes and draws its legs in and up for the next kick

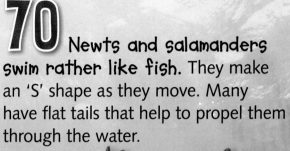
Eastern newt

▲▼ Newts are good swimmers and spend most of their lives in water.

Rough-skinned newt

▼ Green turtles took to the sea about 150 million years ago.

72 A swimming snake may seem unlikely, but most snakes are experts in the water. Sea snakes can stay submerged for five hours and move rapidly through the water. European grass snakes are also good swimmers. They have to be because they eat animals that live around water.

▼ Sea snakes return to land to lay eggs.

Yellow-bellied sea snake

73 Sea turtles have light, flat shells so they can move along more easily under water. Some have managed speeds of 29 kilometres an hour. Their flipper-like front legs 'fly' through the water. Their back legs form mini rudders for steering.

Banded sea snake

Nature's tanks

A giant tortoise can support a one tonne weight. This means that it could be used as a jack to lift up a car — but far kinder and easier simply to go to a local garage!

74 Tortoises and turtles are like armoured tanks — slow but well-protected by their shells. Tortoises live on land and eat mainly plants. Some turtles live in the salty sea, most of which are flesh-eaters. Other turtles, some of which are called terrapins, live in freshwater lakes and rivers.

◀ An eagle's huge talons grip onto a tortoise. The bird will fly with the tortoise, then drop it from a height to break its tough shell.

75 When danger threatens, tortoises can quickly retreat into their mobile homes. They simply draw their head, tail and legs into their shell.

▶ A tortoise's shell is part of its body. It is attached to its skeleton.

76 Tortoises and turtles are ancient members of the reptile world. They are the oldest living reptiles, and might have been around with the very first dinosaurs, about 200 million years ago. They also live longer than almost any other animal – some for up to 150 years!

Indian softshell turtle

Leopard tortoise

Matamata turtle

Hawksbill turtle

▲ Tortoises and turtles belong to a group of reptiles called Chelonians. They all have four limbs, a hard shell and a horny beak for a mouth. Their shells can be leathery or covered in plates.

77 Some sea turtles are among nature's greatest travellers. The green turtle migrates an amazing 2000 kilometres from its feeding grounds off the coast of Brazil to breeding sites such as Ascension Island, in the South Atlantic.

Dangerous enemies

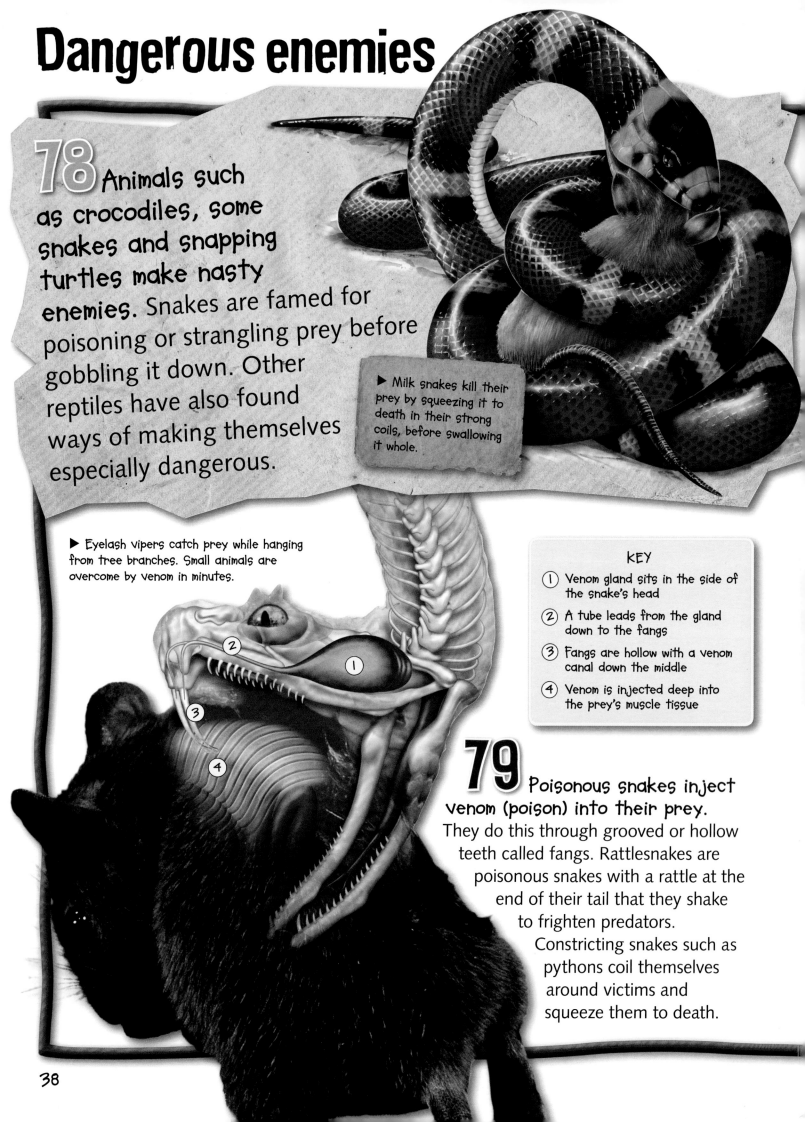

78 Animals such as crocodiles, some snakes and snapping turtles make nasty enemies. Snakes are famed for poisoning or strangling prey before gobbling it down. Other reptiles have also found ways of making themselves especially dangerous.

▶ Milk snakes kill their prey by squeezing it to death in their strong coils, before swallowing it whole.

▶ Eyelash vipers catch prey while hanging from tree branches. Small animals are overcome by venom in minutes.

KEY

① Venom gland sits in the side of the snake's head

② A tube leads from the gland down to the fangs

③ Fangs are hollow with a venom canal down the middle

④ Venom is injected deep into the prey's muscle tissue

79 Poisonous snakes inject venom (poison) into their prey. They do this through grooved or hollow teeth called fangs. Rattlesnakes are poisonous snakes with a rattle at the end of their tail that they shake to frighten predators. Constricting snakes such as pythons coil themselves around victims and squeeze them to death.

QUIZ

1. How does an alligator snapping turtle lure its prey?
2. How do poisonous snakes inject venom (poison) into their prey?
3. Which amphibian has bright yellow spots or stripes?

Answers:
1. By waving the tip of its tongue, which looks like a juicy worm 2. Through grooved or hollow teeth called fangs 3. A fire salamander

▼ Alligator snapping turtles can deliver one of the strongest bites in the animal world.

80 The alligator snapping turtle looks like a rough rock as it lies on the ocean floor. This cunning turtle has an extra trick up its sleeve. The tip of its tongue looks like a juicy worm, which it waves at passing prey to lure it into its jaws.

BEWARE! POISONOUS

▶ A fire salamander sprays foul poisons at a predator.

◀ The skin of a strawberry poison–dart frog is coated with deadly poison.

81 Bright patterns on some amphibians' skin warn predators. Their skin may be foul-tasting or cause irritation. Arrow-poison frogs from South America's rainforests have very bright colours, while fire salamanders have bright yellow spots or stripes.

Clever mimics

82 Reptiles and amphibians are masters of disguise. Some blend into their surroundings naturally, while others can change their appearance – perfect for avoiding predators or sneaking up on prey.

83 Frogs and toads are experts in the art of camouflage (blending with surroundings). Many are coloured shades of green or green-brown, to look just like leaves, grass or tree bark.

▶ A mossy frog's coloured and bumpy skin helps it blend into a tree trunk's mottled surface.

ANIMAL DISGUISE

Make a mask of your favourite reptile or amphibian from a round piece of card or a paper plate. Look at the pictures in this book to help you add details and colour it in. Carefully cut some eye holes, and then attach some string or elastic to the sides to hold it to your head.

84 Many lizards have green or brown camouflage colouring. The chameleon lizard can also change its colour. If it meets an enemy while it is walking along a branch, it can crouch down, stay very still and make itself look like the leaves and bark.

85 The fire-bellied toad has a bright red tummy! It uses it to distract its enemies. When it is threatened, the toad leaps away to safety, and the quick flash of bright red confuses the attacker, giving the toad an extra fraction of a second to escape.

► A flash of this toad's red belly scares and confuses a predator.

► Look closely at this wrinkled dead leaf and you will see it is really a living animal — a fantastic leaf-tail gecko.

86 Some snakes can even pretend to be dead. They lie coiled up with their tongue hanging out, so that predators look elsewhere for a meal.

◄ Some snakes 'play dead' to trick a predator into leaving them alone.

Escape artists

87 Reptiles and amphibians must fight to survive in the deadly natural world. They might make a tasty meal for a predator, unless they have a clever trick or two. Gila monsters, for example, can deliver deadly bites packed with venom.

▶ A gila monster must bite and chew to release its venom.

88 Some salamanders and lizards have detachable tails. If a predator grabs a five-lined tree skink lizard by the tail, it will be left holding a twitching blue tail! The tail does grow back.

89 Spraying an attacker with blood is a good trick. Desert horned lizards puff themselves up, hiss and squirt blood out of their eyes when they are scared.

◀ A desert horned lizard's bloody face is fearsome.

► A skink could make a juicy snack for a bigger animal.

90
A young blue-tongued skink uses colour as a delay tactic. The lizard simply flashes its bright blue tongue and mouth lining at an enemy. The startled predator lets its prey slip away.

91
The Australian shingleback lizard has a tail shaped like a head. By the time a confused predator has worked this one out, the lizard has made its getaway.

▼ Can you tell which end is the shingleback lizard's head?

92
Rattlesnakes are dangerous reptiles. They shake the rattles on their tails to warn attackers before they strike. Their long fangs pump deadly venom deep into the flesh.

◄ A rattlesnake's rattle is formed of layers of dried, moulted skin.

Mega reptiles

93 Dinosaurs were reptiles that roamed the land millions of years ago. Today, our largest reptiles are much smaller than some of them, but they are still savage killers. Crocodiles, alligators and Komodo dragons are powerful hunters with keen senses.

Pointed snout

Fourth tooth on lower jaw sticks out

▲ Most crocodiles live in Africa or Asia.

◄ Alligators live in the Americas and China.

Shorter, more rounded snout

Lower teeth hidden when mouth is closed

94 Crocodiles and alligators usually measure between 3 and 7 metres long — although even bigger ones have been seen. They have thick, leathery skin, huge jaws and a killer instinct. Crocodiles have two big teeth on their lower jaws that can be seen even when their mouth is shut.

95 Komodo dragons are monitor lizards and the largest, heaviest lizards on Earth. They can grow to be about 3 metres in length and reach a weight of 70 kilograms or more. Komodos live on a few islands in Indonesia, where they are protected as so few of them are left in the wild. They can live for 40 years.

◄ Like other lizards, Komodo dragons flick their long tongues in the air so they can 'taste' and smell animals or food nearby. They are fearless predators and hunt snakes, rats, pigs and deer.

96 Baby Komodos live in trees so their parents don't eat them! As soon as they hatch from their eggs, baby Komodos must survive without help from their parents.

Reptiles in danger

97 One-third of all reptiles and amphibians are at risk of dying out forever. They are at risk of extinction because they are losing their habitats (homes) or because they have been hunted.

98 Green turtles may die out because people steal their eggs to sell as food. Their breeding beaches have also been taken over by hotels or houses, or ruined with pollution. Adult green turtles are captured in the seas around Asia and then eaten.

▶ Scientists hope to save green turtles from extinction. They tag them and follow their movements across the oceans.

Geochelone abingdoni
R.I.P
24 de Junio 2012 | June 24th 2012

Solitario George | Lonesome George

Prometemos contar tu historia | We promise to tell your story
y transmitir tu mensaje de conservación | and to share your conservation message.

99 Lonesome George was a type of giant tortoise and the last of his kind. He lived on the Galapagos Islands, where turtles were once common reptiles. When he died in 2012, George's sub-species became extinct forever.

▲ Lonesome George's death has inspired many people to save the last giant tortoises.

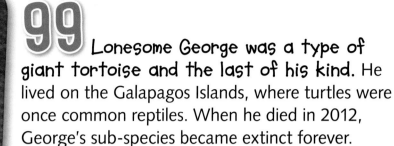

100 Amphibians are at risk from climate change. They need their homes to stay warm and damp, but pollution is changing our planet's weather systems. Many frogs and toads have also died from a skin disease that has spread around the world.

▲ Panamanian golden frogs are probably extinct in the wild.

QUIZ

1. In what year did Lonesome George die?
2. How are scientists trying to save green turtles from extinction?
3. Which frogs are probably extinct in the wild?

Answers:
1. 2012 2. By tagging them and following their movements across the oceans 3. Panamanian golden frogs

Index

Page numbers in **bold** refer to main entries, those in *italics* refer to illustrations